A GIANT LOVE STORY
Original Icelandic title: *Ástarsaga úr fjöllunum*
Text © Guðrún Helgadóttir 1981
Illustrations © Brian Pilkington 1981
English translation © Christopher Sanders 1986
Printing: Prentmiðlun / Hungary

Vaka-Helgafell
Reykjavík 2015

ISBN 978-9979-2-1374-1

Vaka-Helgafell is an imprint of ◊ Forlagið ehf.
www.forlagid.is

A GIANT
LOVE STORY

By Guðrún Helgadóttir
Illustrations by Brian Pilkington

Vaka-Helgafell

"Is it true, Dad?" said Ari. "Is it true that there are giants who steal naughty children and carry them into the mountains?"

"No, no," said his father. "Giants have more than enough unruly children of their own."

"Tell me a story about the giants," said Ari. He settled himself on a rock that he and his father called the "story stone".

His father raised an eyebrow. "Wouldn't you rather hear about elves, Ari? I thought you were afraid of giants."
This was true. Ari was terrified of giants. His father wasn't, though. He was afraid of other things – landslides, earthquakes, and volcanoes. But these sorts of things became bothersome only every now and then. The giants were there all the time, up in the mountains.

"The giants are huge, aren't they?" asked Ari. "Are they as big as this rock?"

"Oh, much bigger," Dad answered. "Why, one of the sheep here would fit nicely into the palm of a giant's hand."

"As big as that!" Ari gasped. "And to think that there's a giant in every one of Iceland's mountains …"

"Yes, that is true. But the giants only come out after dark. Sunshine turns them to stone."

"I've heard that there are giant old hags that put human children like me in a sack and carry them off to their homes in the mountains," Ari said, shivering.

"I doubt that," said Dad. "Giants are too lazy and dim-witted to carry out such a plan. Flumbra didn't have even enough sense to carry her own children in a sack. Yes, that is what she should have done."

"Flumbra? Who is Flumbra, Dad?"

"She was a giantess."

"Tell me about her," Ari said as he moved closer to his father. And Dad began.

Once upon a time, the giantess Flumbra fell head-over-heels in love with an ugly giant who lived far, far away on the other side of the mountains. Now, all giants are lazy, but Flumbra's giant was lazy beyond compare. He was so lazy that he couldn't even be bothered to visit her.

Flumbra waited and waited for him. She even started to clean up her cave – for the first time in a hundred years – just in case he might show up. Everything that was lying around loose she threw out of the cave. Soon gravel, then stones, and finally boulders began to bounce and slide down the mountainside, pulling up flowers, grass, and moss all along the way.

"It's a landslide!" said the people in the villages below.

Flumbra had not cooked a hot meal for a hundred years. Giants rarely do any cooking at all. But after cleaning out her cave, Flumbra felt terribly hungry.

So she puffed at the old coals on the hearth until they began to glow, and soon flames licked the cauldron. As the stew boiled and bubbled, great pillars of steam billowed out of Flumbra's cave. Soot and ashes rained down on the valleys and sent the sheep scuttling home with blackened faces.

"The volcano is erupting!" shouted the terrified people.

Flumbra gobbled up as much stew as a whole village of ordinary people could eat. But even though she was plump and pretty, still her lazy giant didn't come to see her. So she would have to go to him.

Flumbra waited until dark. Then off she lumbered to see her giant. She had to move quickly and get to his cave before sunrise or else she would turn to stone. Fortunately, it was wintertime, when the days are short and night wonderfully long.

Sweating and panting, she galloped across mountains and moors to meet her ugly giant. Lazy though he was, the minute he saw Flumbra, the giant couldn't help but be head-over-heels in love with her, too. They hugged and they kissed. They jumped on each other and rolled around together so that everything shook. The earth began to quake all the way down to the sea. Houses started to crack and crumble. Power lines snapped, and the lights went out.

"An earthquake!" shouted the people as they ran out of their houses.

Only one thing could come out of such a fuss. And one
night, Flumbra gave birth to eight sons. They were big and
unbelievably ugly, very much like their father.

Flumbra thought they were beautiful, and she loved them
so dearly that she quivered and shook. She caused such a
commotion that the little birch bushes on the mountainside
rustled far into the night.

The baby giants wailed so loudly that the noise echoed
through the mountains and valleys, but Flumbra didn't notice.

She simply stared at her children, amazed at how beautiful they were with their fuzzy faces and strands of coarse, yellow hair. She had never seen such beautiful babies in all of Iceland.

Flumbra had to find a beautiful name for every one of them. But how could she find names for so many? She racked her brain day and night. Down by the sea, the people heard a low moaning from the hills as Flumbra thought and thought.

"Whatever is going to happen next?" they said as they pulled the bedclothes up over their heads.

Flumbra didn't give up until she had found names for all eight of her sons. They yelled as though their lungs would burst when she told them what they were to be called. But Flumbra couldn't have been happier.

The first was called Altogether-Beautiful. The second was called Completely-Beautiful, and the third, Even-more-Beautiful. The fourth was called A-Little-Bit-Beautiful, the fifth, Almost-as-Beautiful, the sixth, A-Wee-Shade-Beautiful, and the seventh, Every-Bit-As-Beautiful. The eighth was called Absolutely-Beautiful.

The giantess was indeed proud of her eight sons. All through the day and all through the night she nursed her little giants. She had so much milk that, even when her sons had drunk their fill, it trickled in whitish-blue streams out of the cave and flowed down the mountainside to the cream-coloured lake below.

"Oh, look!" said the people. "Mountain milk." And they took pictures of the streams with their cameras.

At first, Flumbra was so busy nursing her babies that she had no time to think of the giant she was so head-over-heels in love with. But one mild spring evening, Flumbra's milk was all gone. It was then that she remembered the giant who was the father of her eight sons. Suddenly, she just had to go and see him.

So once again, Flumbra prepared for the long journey to visit him. This time, though, she had to take her eight sons with her over the mountains and moors, across the streams

and gullies. Poor, poor Flumbra – to be so much in love with such a great big, ugly giant, who lived so far away!

Flumbra set out the moment the sun went down behind the hills. She strode away as fast as she could with eight sons dawdling along behind her. They shouted and hooted, but she hurriedly pulled them along. Sometimes she would swing all eight at once, in a long line of baby giants, across glaciers, wide rivers, and deep valleys. Even so, the trip took longer than when Flumbra had gone alone.

Alas, Flumbra never reached her beloved giant, for when she was almost there, the sun peeped up over the edge of the sea, and she and her eight sons turned to stone.

They stand there still, Flumbra and her boys, up on the mountaintop. They will stand there for thousands of years to come, as landmarks. Even if Flumbra's ugly giant stomped right past them, he would never recognize Flumbra. And he never knew he was the father of eight little giants.

Flumbra and her sons are never lonely up there in the mountains. In the spring, arctic terns come to spend the summer. Sometimes they lay eggs in Flumbra's ears and fill them with the chatter of their baby birds.

Nature is kind to those stone giants. She slowly wraps them in clothes of moss and heather, grass and lichen. Altogether-Beautiful and Completely-Beautiful, Even-More-Beautiful and A-Little-Bit-Beautiful, Almost-as-Beautiful and A-Wee-Shade-Beautiful, and Every-Bit-as-Beautiful and Absolutely-Beautiful grow more beautiful every year. Their untidy hair has long since turned to mounds of moss where buttercups and bluebells grow in summer. And Flumbra is adorned like Mother Iceland herself with small patches of grass and flowers crowning her head.

When the weather gets cold, Flumbra and her boys are
muffled in soft snow. Only their cheeks and noses are bare,
but their fuzzy faces never freeze. Flumbra is quite handsome
in her white coat and matching cap. Her beloved giant ought
to see her now. He wouldn't believe his eyes!

"And that, Ari, is the story of Flumbra the giantess," Dad finished.

"Do you know where they are now?" asked Ari.

"No, but maybe we'll find them some day when we are out in the mountains. And if we do, we must remember to tell Flumbra how beautiful her children are."

Ari knew exactly what he would do if he found Flumbra and her little giants. First he would crawl up and make his way across the shoulders of the little giants, taking care not to disturb their flowers and moss, until he could finally climb up onto the crown of Flumbra's head.

Then Ari would pat Flumbra gently and say, "How very silly you were, you old giantess. How gigantically silly. You should have carried your sons in a sack. Then you would have reached your lazy giant before the sunlight caught you."

To this day, Ari's father is afraid of earthquakes and landslides and volcanoes. But Ari isn't afraid of giants – not any more.